Cinderellaphant

Cinderellaphant

By Dianne de Las Casas
Illustrated by Stefan Jolet

PELICAN PUBLISHING COMPANY

GRETNA 2014

For my mom, Josie, Chretien, who always sparkles in my eyes
—Dianne de Las Casas

Library of Congress Cataloging-in-Publication Data

De Las Casas, Dianne.
  Cinderellaphant / by Dianne de Las Casas ; illustrated by Stefan Jolet.
      pages cm
  Summary: An adaptation of the traditional tale of Cinderella with animals rather than humans as characters.
  ISBN 978-1-4556-1900-9 (hardcover : alk. paper)—ISBN 978-1-4556-1901-6 (e-book) [1. Fairy tales. 2. Folklore--France.] I. Jolet, Stefan, illustrator. II. Perrault, Charles, 1628-1703. Cendrillon. III. Cinderella. English. IV. Title.
  PZ8.D3735Cin 2014
  398.20944--dc23
  [E]

2013036409

Printed in Malaysia
Published by Pelican Publishing Company, Inc.
1000 Burmaster Street, Gretna, Louisiana 70053

In an animal kingdom far away, there lived a pretty pachyderm with a big heart. Her name was . . .

Ellaphant.

She lived with her stepmother and two step-hippos. Hippolotta was a bratty bully and Hippolene was a mega meanie. They made her clean the cinders from the fireplace and they called her "Cinderellaphant."

Cinderellaphant was as busy as a beaver. She cleaned from sunup to sundown. Her step-hippos flaunted their fancy frocks while Cinderellaphant wore rags covered in soot. She often felt irrelephant.

One day, Cinderellaphant heard a beastly screech. She ran into the kitchen and saw Hippolotta jump on the kitchen table. Hippolene swatted a newspaper in the air and shrieked. "It's so gross!"

Cinderellaphant saw a poor church mouse quivering on the floor. She quickly scooped up the little mouse and said, "Run away!" The mouse wiggled her whiskers and scurried off. Cinderellaphant smiled.

One morning, a royal messenger announced, "The Prince seeks a bride. Every maiden in the kingdom must attend the Royal Ball at the King's Castle on Saturday night at seven o'clock!"

Hippolotta grabbed the invitation. "Shut up! Baboon 5 is playing at the ball!"

Hippolene snatched the scroll from her sister, "Oh my gosh! I just go ape over that band!" The step-hippos chattered on and on about what to wear.

Cinderellaphant's heart leapt for joy. What would she wear?! Then her stepmother spoke, "Cinderellaphant, you cannot attend the ball. You have a lion's share of work to do."

Hours before the ball, Hippolotta badgered, "Press my dress!" Hippolene bellowed, "Shine my shoes!" Cinderellaphant tried to do everything at once.

Finally, Cinderellaphant's stepmother and step-hippos were ready. They stampeded past her and roared away in their fancy ride.

Cinderellaphant had to hurry. She opened a cedar chest. "Wow!" she cried. "Look at all the junk in this trunk!" Finally, she found what she was looking for. She tried on the dress but it was a tad petite for the Rubenesque beauty. Cinderellaphant blubbered.

RIIIP!

"Cinderellaphant, dry your tears," comforted a winged-mouse. "I am your fairy godmouse. I am here to repay your kindness when you rescued me in the kitchen."

"What do you mean?" asked Cinderellaphant.

"This!" The fairy godmouse swished her wand and Cinderellaphant was bedecked in a bedazzling ball gown and sparkling glass slippers. Then the fairy godmouse said, "Quickly, dear, run into the garden and get me a peanut!"

Cinderellaphant returned with the nut. With a swirl of her wand, the fairy godmouse transformed the peanut into a carriage befitting a princess.

The little mouse tutted, "Make haste to the ball. You have little time. Riches will be rags when you hear the midnight chime. Now drive them nuts, girl!"

Cinderellaphant hugged her fairy godmouse. "Thank you!" She climbed into her carriage and sped away.

When Cinderellaphant entered the castle, every creature exclaimed, "Who is that elephant in the room?!"
Immediately, the Prince beheld the exquisite animal. He asked for a dance.

The prince would not leave Cinderellaphant's side even after she stomped on his toes and twirled him across the room, sending him crashing into the buffet.

He said, "You are as strong as an ox! I love it!" No one else could get a dance with the prince. Hippolotta and Hippolene fumed.

Cinderellaphant and the prince boogied and hoofed it all night long. She was having a whale of a time! They did the bunny hop.

They danced the foxtrot.

They even tangoed toe to toe.

BONG!
BONG!
BONG!

But then the clock struck midnight.

Cinderellaphant panicked. "I have to go!" As fast as a cheetah, she raced down the castle stairs.

The prince cried, "Wait!" But it was too late. Cinderellaphant vanished, leaving only one colossal glass slipper sparkling on the stairs.

The prince picked it up and proclaimed, "Only the maiden whose foot fits this sizeable slipper shall be my bride." He began a kingdom-wide search.

Every maiden in the kingdom tried on the shoe but it was hopeless. Finally, the prince arrived at Cinderellaphant's house. Hippolotta and Hippolene both stretched out their feet, but no matter how much they wiggled, waggled, and wriggled, the gargantuan glass slipper did not fit.

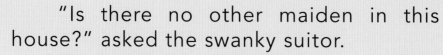

"Is there no other maiden in this house?" asked the swanky suitor.

Cinderellaphant swelled with courage and said quietly, "I haven't tried it on."

Her stepmother protested, "She is nothing but a maid servant!"

The prince emphasized, "Every maiden tries on the slipper." He beckoned the bashful beauty.

Cinderellaphant put her best foot forward. The shiny shoe fit! She reached into her pocket and pulled out the matching sparkling slipper.

"No! No! No!" Hippolotta and Hippolene threw terrible temper tantrums.

The prince smiled at Cinderellaphant. "Being a princess is an enormous job and you're the only maiden big enough to fill a princess' shoes."

Cinderellaphant had found her sole mate! She and the prince were, of course, married. The pachyderm princess and the royal roan honeymooned in the tropics where they tangoed toe to toe. And they lived hoofily ever after.

Author's Note

Cinderella is my all-time-favorite fairy tale. I have always wanted to write a twist on the traditional tale of Cinderella and many years ago, the idea for "Cinderellaphant" popped into my head and stuck. Plus, I love big bling and fabulous footwear! The animals in this story are so amusing. I love Stefan Jolet's Hilarious sense of humor. Baboon 5 is definitely one of my favorite bands!